A QUESTION AND ANSWER STORYBOOK

Why do Cows Moo?

and other farm animal questions

by Catherine Ripley

illustrated by Scot Ritchie

Owl

Why do Cows Moo? and other farm animal questions

Owl Books are published by Greey de Pencier Books Inc.,
179 John Street, Suite 500, Toronto, Ontario M5T 3G5

The Owl colophon is a trademark of Owl Children's Trust Inc.
Greey de Pencier Books Inc. is a licensed user of trademarks of Owl Children's Trust Inc.

Distributed in the United States by Firefly Books (U.S.) Inc.,
230 Fifth Avenue, Suite 1607, New York, NY 10001.

We acknowledge the generous support of the Canada Council
for the Arts and the Ontario Arts Council for our publishing program.

Special thanks to the children of Terrace, Kitimat and Prince Rupert (British Columbia) for some great questions about farm animals, to the Canadian Children's Book Centre for sending me there during Children's Book Week (1996) and to the Canada Council for their support of this annual event. Also, thank you to Kerry Carnegie, Ontario Ministry of Agriculture, Food, and Rural Affairs; Michel Charon, Agriculture Museum, National Museum of Science and Technology; *Chickadee* Magazine; Blair Dow (sheep); Kevin Ferguson (chickens); Barb Fraser (cows); Michel Gosselin (birds), Canadian Museum of Nature; John Hendriks (pigs); Bob McClelland, Central Experimental Farm, Agriculture and Agri-Food Canada; Terry McEvoy (bees); Mickie Moir (rabbits); Donna Naughton (mammals), the Canadian Museum of Nature; Marion Newman, Chair, Agriculture Awareness Committee for Ottawa-Carleton; Ontario Arts Council; Bruce Ripley; and Susan Woodward (mammals), Royal Ontario Museum. And once again, thank you to Sheba and Kat (editors), Mary (designer), and Scot (illustrator) — half a dozen and counting!

DEDICATION

**With the highest respect for farmers everywhere.
Also, in memory of Cardinal Hill Orchards (1982–1992),
and all of Bruce's hard work in revitalizing a farm.**

Cataloguing in Publication Data

Ripley, Catherine, 1957–
Why do cows moo? and other farm animal questions

(A question and answer storybook)
ISBN 1-895688-77-9 (bound) ISBN 1-895688-78-7 (pbk.)

1. Domestic animals – Miscellanea – Juvenile literature.
I. Ritchie, Scot. II. Title. III. Series: Ripley,
Catherine, 1957–   . Question and answer storybook.

SF75.5.R56 1998   j636   C97-931759-2

Design & Art Direction: Mary Opper

Also available:
Why is Soap so Slippery? and other bathtime questions
Do the Doors Open by Magic? and other supermarket questions
Why do Stars Twinkle? and other nighttime questions
Why is the Sky Blue? and other outdoor questions
Why Does Popcorn Pop? and other kitchen questions

Printed in Hong Kong

A   B   C   D   E   F

Contents

Why do ducks waddle?

They'd rather be swimming than walking around! A duck's body is wide. Its legs are far apart and back near its tail. Its feet are webbed. Perfect for swimming — which ducks do a lot of the time — but not so good for walking. Waddle, waddle, splash!

How does a chick get out of the egg?

It pecks its way out. After 21 days inside an egg, a chick gets big. It needs more space, and is ready to breathe fresh air. Using its egg tooth, a special bump on the end of its beak, it pecks a tiny hole. Peck, peck, peck . . . finally the egg starts to crack. Chip, pip, peck! A few hours later, out comes a tired, wet chick. Soon the chick is dry and fluffy, and a day later its egg tooth falls off.

Why does a bunny's fur feel so soft?

Each hair is thin and bends easily. That's why it's soft. Rabbits have two types of hair: short underfur and guard hairs on top. The shorter the guard hairs, the softer they feel. When a rabbit is sick, its fur can be dry and rough. So you're petting a healthy, short-haired rabbit.

What's a ewe?

A mother sheep. A father sheep is called a ram, and a baby sheep is called a lamb. We give male, female and young animals different names. How many of these animal names do you know?

SHEEP
Ram, Ewe, Lamb

EWES AND LAMBS

SHEEP SHEARING

DUCKS
Drake, Duck, Duckling

GEESE
Gander, Goose, Gosling

CHICKENS
Rooster, Hen, Chick

RABBITS
Buck, Doe, Kit

TURKEYS
Tom, Hen, Poult

COWS
Bull, Cow, Calf

HORSES
Stallion, Mare, Foal

BEES
Queen bee,
Drone (male),
Worker (female),
Larva (young)

GOATS
Billy, Nanny, Kid

PIGS
Boar, Sow, Piglet

Why are sheep shaved?

To keep them cool and clean, and to get the wool to sell. It's hard to shear the wool off in one big piece! The wool is washed, untangled and spun into long strands of yarn — sometimes by hand, but usually in big machines. The yarn can be knitted or woven into clothes or blankets. During the year the sheep grow back their woolen coats and then — baaaa! — it's sheep shearing time again in the spring.

Why do cows moo?

They're talking! One way animals talk to each other is by making sounds — baaa-ing, quacking, woofing, oinking and moooooo-ing. Dairy cows moo or "bawl" if milking time is late, to tell the farmer their udders are getting too full of milk. They also moo if they're hungry. Out in the pasture, beef cows with calves moo to keep their babies close and safe.

What are the cows chewing?

Their cuds. A cow eats hay, grain or grass. Its huge stomach has four parts. The food is formed into balls or cuds in the second part, the reticulum. Muscles there move and send the cuds, one by one, back to the cow's mouth. Chew, chew! The cow breaks down the cuds, then swallows again. Now the well-chewed food moves on through the rest of the cow's stomach.

Reticulum   Rumen   Omasum   Abomasum

Why do horses swish their tails?

To flick away the flies. Horn flies, stable flies, horse flies, house flies, black flies, mosquitoes and other insects all bother and bite horses. Bzzz! Bite! Sometimes the insects can pass on germs that make horses sick. So the horse uses its tail to keep the flies from landing on its skin.

Why do horses sleep standing up?

For a fast getaway. Today, most horses live in stables. But long ago they all lived in the wild. They were hunted by wolves, mountain lions, coyotes and bears. To stay safe and alive, horses had to be able to run away from danger FAST! Just two hours after a foal is born, it is ready to run. Horses can take off faster from a standing-up position than from a lying-down position, and that's why horses sleep standing up.

Why do only some goats have horns?

Because they haven't been de-horned. Many goats are born ready to grow horns. Horns are hard and have no feeling — sort of like your fingernails. In the wild, goats use them to protect themselves, to show off and to fight. But on a farm, sharp horns can be dangerous to people and other animals. When kids are a few days old, many farmers stop the horns from starting to grow.

How do bees make honey?

They dry out nectar. Nectar is sweet, watery liquid that bees collect from flowers. The bees take the nectar to the hive to be put in tiny openings in the honeycomb called cells. Bees fan the nectar with their wings. They stir it and move it from cell to cell, mixing it with older nectar. As the nectar slowly dries, it thickens. Then, when the cell is full, the bee seals it off with a wax cap. Mmmmm, honey!

Why do pigs roll in the mud?

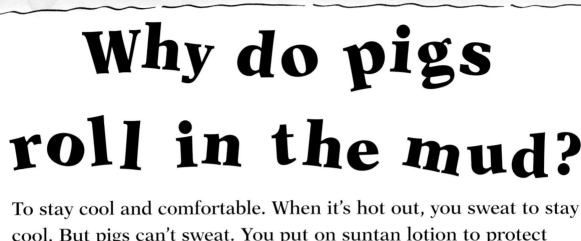

To stay cool and comfortable. When it's hot out, you sweat to stay cool. But pigs can't sweat. You put on suntan lotion to protect your skin from burning and use bug stuff for the bugs, but pigs can't do that. The barn keeps animals cool, clean and bug-free, but what do pigs do outside? Roll in the mud! It protects their skin from sunburn and bug bites, and it keeps them cool, too.

Farm Bits

Is that chicken eating dirt? A chicken doesn't have teeth to grind up its food. So it swallows stones and bits of dirt. In a part of the chicken called the gizzard, the stones grind and mash down the food the chicken has swallowed.

Rabbits are always wiggling their noses. In the wild, rabbits need to be on the lookout for danger. They use their long ears to hear every sound, and move their noses to catch smells from every direction. Wiggle, twitch.

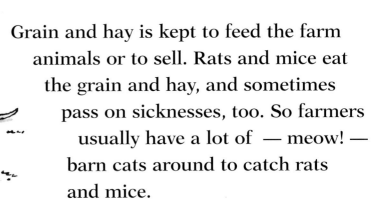

Grain and hay is kept to feed the farm animals or to sell. Rats and mice eat the grain and hay, and sometimes pass on sicknesses, too. So farmers usually have a lot of — meow! — barn cats around to catch rats and mice.